BABY'S
MOTHER GOOSE

BABY'S
Mother Goose

Illustrated by Eloise Wilkin

 **GOLDEN PRESS**
Western Publishing Company, Inc.
Racine, Wisconsin

Ninth Printing, 1978

0-307-10411-7

London Bridge

London Bridge is falling down,
Falling down, falling down,

London Bridge is falling down,
My fair lady.

Build it up with iron bars,
Iron bars, iron bars,

Build it up with iron bars,
My fair lady.

Little Girl with the Curl

There was a little girl,
Who had a little curl

Right in the middle of her forehead;

When she was good,
She was very, very good,

But when she was bad
she was horrid.

Pat-a-Cake

Pat-a-cake, pat-a-cake,
  baker's man!
Bake me a cake
  as fast as you can;
Roll it and pat it
  and mark it with "B,"
And put it in the oven
  for baby and me.

Jack and Jill

Jack and Jill went up the hill
To fetch a pail of water;
Jack fell down
And broke his crown,
And Jill came tumbling after.

Then up Jack got, and home did trot,
As fast as he could caper.
They put him to bed and plastered his head
With vinegar and brown paper.

Baa, Baa, Black Sheep

Baa, baa, black sheep,
Have you any wool?

Yes, sir, yes, sir,
Three bags full.
One for master,
One for my dame,
And one for the little boy
That lives in the lane.

Tom, Tom, the Piper's Son

Tom, Tom, the piper's son
Stole a pig and away he run.
The pig was eat and Tom was beat,
And Tom went crying down the street.

Tom, Tom, the piper's son,
He learned to play when he was young;
But all the tunes that he could play
Was "Over the hills and far away."

Little Miss Muffet

Little Miss Muffet
She sat on a tuffet,
Eating of curds and whey;

There came a great spider,
Who sat down beside her,
And frightened Miss Muffet away.

The North Wind

The north wind doth blow,
And we shall have snow,
And what will the robin do then,
  Poor thing?

He'll sit in the barn
And keep himself warm,
And hide his head under his wing,
  Poor thing!

Jack, Be Nimble

Jack, be nimble,

Jack, be quick,

Jack, jump over the candlestick.

Little Jack Horner

Little Jack Horner

Sat in the corner

Eating a Christmas pie;

He put in his thumb,

And pulled out a plum,

And said,

"What a good boy am I!"

Mistress Mary

Mistress Mary, quite contrary,
How does your garden grow?
With cockle shells and silver bells
And pretty maids all in a row.

Mary Had a Little Lamb

Mary had a little lamb,
Its fleece was white as snow,

And everywhere that Mary went
The lamb was sure to go.

It followed her to school one day,
Which was against the rule:

It made the children laugh and play
To see a lamb at school.

Little Boy Blue

Little Boy Blue,
 come blow your horn!
The sheep's in the meadow,
 the cow's in the corn.
Where's the boy
 that looks after the sheep?
He's under the haycock,
 fast asleep.
Will you wake him?
 No, not I;
For if I do,
 he'll be sure to cry.

What

Are

Little

Boys

Made

of?

What are little boys made of, made of?
What are little boys made of?
Frogs and snails, and puppy-dogs' tails;
That's what little boys are made of.

What are little girls made of, made of?
What are little girls made of?
Sugar and spice, and all things nice;
That's what little girls are made of.

Bobby Shaftoe

Bobby Shaftoe's gone to sea,
Silver buckles on his knee;
He'll come back and marry me,
Pretty Bobby Shaftoe.

Bobby Shaftoe's fat and fair,
Combing down his yellow hair;
He's my love for evermore,
Pretty Bobby Shaftoe.

Pease Porridge Hot

Pease porridge hot,
  Pease porridge cold,
Pease porridge in the pot,
  Nine days old.

    Some like it hot,
     Some like it cold,
    Some like it in the pot,
     Nine days old.

Little Bo-Peep

Little Bo-Peep
  has lost her sheep,
    And can't tell
      where to find them;
        Leave them alone,
          and they'll come home,
            And bring their tails behind them.